Magnificent Me Magnificent You
The Great Barrier Reef

Dedicated to my sons, Christopher and Ethan, and all the children of the world.

Know you are magnificent.

Treasure our magnificent planet earth.

First Published by Magnificent Me Magnificent You Ltd 2021
www.magnificentmemagnificentyou.com

Distributed Globally, email info@magnificentmemagnificentyou.com for details of trade distributors in your region

Text copyright Dawattie Basdeo © 2021

ISBN: 978-1-7398804-0-8

A CIP catalogue record for this book is available from the British library.

Author: Dawattie Basdeo
www.magnificentmemagnificentyou.com

Story Illustrator: Chantelle Thaller
Instagram: @sakura.customs
www.sakuracustoms.com

Activities Illustrator: Anna Stothart

Public Liability Disclaimer
The author nor the publisher cannot accept responsibility for, or shall be liable for, any accident, or injury, loss or damage, including any consequential loss that results from using the ideas, information, procedures or advise offered in this book.

Contents Page

It was the dawn of a new day.

Outside the sun is rising and the birds are singing their morning songs.

Twins Crystal and Leo are gently awakened from their sleep by the warm rays of the morning sun dancing on their faces and the happy chirps of the birds outside their window.

Leo is the first to jump out of bed. both Crystal and Leo choose to start their day with some exercise.

They do a round of yoga Sun Salutations to waken and energise their body for the day ahead.

They then take turns to use the bathroom to brush their teeth, shower and get dressed for the day.

1

"What shall we do today?" asked Crystal.

"Let's explore mummy's bag of travelling treasures and see what comes out today," said Leo.

Leo put his hand into the bag of travelling treasures and slowly pulled out a most beautiful sea shell.

The shell was smooth, silky and tough and the inside of the shell glistened with a myriad of shiny colours.

Leo held the shell to his ears. "Wow," he exclaimed "I can hear the ocean."

He passed the shell to Crystal, whose face lit up with delight as she placed the shell against her ears and listened to the sound of the ocean.

Crystal said excitedly, "Let's use our wishing mirror to find out where in the world this beautiful shell is from."

Along with their dog Einstein, they both stood in front of their wishing mirror, closed their eyes and said, "Mirror mirror, take us to the home of our shell treasure."

When they opened their eyes, they found they were standing on a golden sandy beach, next to a sparkling turquoise ocean.

They stood with their toes in the ocean and as the water gently massaged their toes, they took in some deep breaths of the warm fresh ocean air.

As they looked out across the ocean, they spotted two dolphins beckoning to them.

"They are calling us," said Crystal, "let's go and see if they need help."

Crystal and Leo dived into the sparkling water and swam to meet the dolphins.

Both dolphins appeared to be well.

The dolphins kept chattering to them and moving their heads to point out to sea.

Crystal peered in the direction the dolphins were pointing.

In the far-off distance, she could see something floating on the water, but because it was so far away, she could not make out exactly what it was.

"I think there is something over there that the dolphins would like us to look at," said Crystal.

"It looks very far from the shore," said Crystal, "do you think we should go so far from the shore?"

Leo said, "Don't worry, dolphins are very friendly and are always rescuing and helping humans, I am sure they won't let any harm come to us."

"Look can you see their dolphin smiles?"

"Mum said, when we connect with our infinite love within, our face always lights up with a smile.
Remember mum's statue of Buddha in meditation, his mouth is turned upwards in a smile because he is a radiant being of love.
Dolphin's smile because they are full of love.
Mum gave me a lovely mantra about smiling,

I Am Love
I Radiate Love To All
With My Smile"

6

Leo continued, "That's why people who are in love smile a lot, because they are connecting with the power of love, their true self.

So, let us trust our dolphin friends and hold onto their backs and let them take us to see what is floating over there. I am sure they will help us get back to shore."

Crystal and Leo held confidently on to the dolphin backs, who swam them to the floating object.

As the dolphins swam, they leaped and dived through the waves laughing and chattering to each other.

Crystal and Leo peered through the sparkling clear water to see what lay below the ocean's surface.

"Wow, look at all the amazing sea life and corals, they are so beautiful.

Look at the funny expressions on the sea turtles faces, look there is Nemo and his friends.

There are so many beautiful colours, it is like an underwater dancing rainbow," laughed Crystal.

"This must be the Great Barrier Reef," said Crystal.
"Mum told me about it, she said it is the only living thing on Earth that can be seen from Space.
"Wow, it is even more spectacular than I imagined."
"I wonder what the dolphins are saying to each other?" said Leo.

"Maybe they are chatting about an ocean party they are going to this evening," Crystal said excitedly.

"Yes," laughed Leo, "that would be fun. I have just thought of a song that we could sing if we were at the party for all the sea animals to dance to."

Leo sang his song of the Dolphins Smile to Crystal.

By the time Leo had finished his song, they had arrived the floating object. It was a boy lying on a surfboard.

"Are you okay?" Asked Crystal.

"I fell off my surfboard and hurt my legs on the corals," muttered the boy. "The next thing I know, I am lying on top of my surfboard and I can see you both coming towards me on the dolphins."

"The pain from hurting your legs must have knocked you out," said Leo, "I am guessing the dolphins must have rescued you and got you back on your surfboard."

"Don't worry," he continued, "the dolphins will help us get you back to shore. You lie flat on your board and hold on tight to it."

The dolphins swam everyone safely back to shore.

As they approached the beach, they could see that clever Einstein, their dog, had fetched help. Standing beside Einstein were two young men who recognised the boy and swam out to meet them and help them ashore.

"What happened?" asked one of the young men.

"I fell off my board and hurt my leg on the coral. I think I must have passed out from the pain, but before I did pass out, I think I saw a most beautiful mermaid coming to my rescue." Replied the boy.

The two young men laughed as they knew their young friend always dreamt of meeting a mermaid. "Well some dreams do come true," they both said.

The young boy thanked Crystal and Leo for rescuing him.

"We were happy to help, but I think we need to thank our friends, the dolphins," said Crystal.

They all stood and waved and shouted, "Thank You" to the dolphins.

The dolphins somersaulted in the air with delight and then swam back out to sea.

Crystal and Leo then said goodbye to the boy and his friends who carried him off to get his leg seen to.

Once the boys had left, all was quiet once more on the beach.

Crystal, Leo and Einstein stood at the water's edge, breathing in the fresh ocean air.

As they stood there they were filled with a feeling of incredible awe at the magnificence and beauty that lay in front of them.

Looking down Crystal spotted in the water, beside her feet, another shell, just like the one they already had, and beside the shell was a Starfish.

Crystal bent down and picked them both up.

She waded into the water and gently placed the starfish far back into the ocean. "I just rescued a Starfish, laughed Crystal, it feels great to help others."

She then returned to Leo on the beach. Smiling at each other, they each held a shell to their ear, closed their eyes and took one last deep breath of the invigorating ocean air.

When they opened their eyes, they were back in their room.

They ran to their Mum, eager to tell her about their adventures. She had been busy working on her laptop so they gave her a needed back massage while sharing all their news.

After they finish recounting their day's adventure, they helped their mum make a delicious healthy dinner which they enjoyed together before their bedtime.

Before going to sleep Crystal and Leo like to say a prayer. Tonight, they chose to say an Australian Peace Prayer **In each of us there is a little of all of us.**

"In each of us there is a little of all of us."

"Face East.

Pray for the dawning of peace around the world

Face South.

Pray for the warming of hearts among enemies

Face West.

Pray for the settling of violence and hostilities

Face North.

Pray for the discovery of our way to Love and Peace"

Crystal and Leo snuggled down into their beds and closed their eyes. Taking deep breaths in and out, they gently relaxed all the muscles in their body, from the tips of their toes to the tops of their heads.

Once they are fully relaxed, they drift off to sleep, dreaming of swimming in the Great Barrier Reef with the dolphins.

End of story

Yoga Activities

- Sun Salutation - Surya Namaskar

- Ocean Breath – Ujjayii Pranayama

- Dolphin Pose – Arda Pincha Mayurasana

- Dolphin Meditation

- Dancing Star Game

- Dolphin Song

- Interesting Facts About The Great Barrier Reef

Wake up and energise your body for the day with yoga sun salutation asana.

2. Breathing out, open your hands out to your sides, palm facing forward, in yoga mountain pose. Stand tall and strong like a mountain.

1. Stand tall, with hands in prayer pose at your heart centre. Breath here and focus on the self, your core, your inner sun.

3. Breathing in, circle your hands up above your head, reaching tall to the sky, look up and reach for your dreams.

6. Breathing out, step your right foot back to join your left foot, forming a straight line with your body, known as yoga Plank pose.

5. Breathing in, straighten your legs, raise your upper torso parallel to the floor, head looking forward. Then step your left foot back into a lunge.

4. Breathing out, flow your arms down in a circle around your body, folding forwards and downwards from your hips bringing your hands to rest on the outside of each foot, with fingers pointing forwards in line with your toes. If needed you can bend your knees slightly. Allow your head to hang towards the floor like a rag doll Feel the earth below you, supporting your every step.

8. Breathing in roll your shoulders back, opening your chest forward. Push down through your arms lifting your chest forward and upwards into Cobra pose. Your legs and belly button remain flat on the floor with soles of feet skywards, take a few breaths here.

7. Breathing out lower your body to yoga Staff pose, your elbows are bent alongside your body, your hands flat on the ground under your shoulders. Your legs parallel to the floor, toes tucked forwards.

9. Breathing out, tuck your toes under to point forwards. Push up equally through your arms and legs to raise your hips skywards, allow your head to flow downwards between your arms in a yoga Downward Dog position. Take a few breaths here.

12. Lower your hands in prayer position to your heart centre. Breathe here, take a moment to think of a few of the things you are grateful for and set your intention for the day ahead. Then repeat the sequence, this time starting with the opposite leg.

11. Breathing in slowly circle your hands up round your body, raising your body to standing tall position with your head coming up last and hands coming to join above the head in prayer position.

10. Breathing in step your right foot forward between your hands, forming a lunge position, then bring your left foot to join forming a forward fold with your body, hands resting on the ground or your shins

As the waves roll up and down, so our breath flows in and out

1. Sit in a comfortable seated position, tall and upright.
Hands gently resting on your lap or in a hand position mudra. A popular mudra is chin mudra, formed by touching the end of the thumb and index finger with palms opening upwards.
Eyes maybe open or closed as you choose.

2. Sit for a moment, breathing at your regular breath and allow your body and mind to relax

3. Now take a deep breath in through your nose, as you exhale round your mouth and flow the breath up along the throat and out through the mouth, making a *HA* sound - as you would breathe when fogging up a mirror.

4. Practice this breath flow technique of fogging up a mirror for a couple of minutes. Observe how the air travels along the back of the throat and out through the rounded mouth making a *HA* sound.

5. Once comfortable with this technique of shaping the flow of breath, close your mouth. Continue breathing using this method... but now allow the exhale to release through the nose.

As the breath flows up along the curved back of the throat and out through the nose, you will observe a gentle ocean sound, as opposed to the *HA* sound when the breath is released through the mouth.

6. Practise breathing using this technique for a few minutes. Breathe in for a count of 2 or 4, whichever feels comfortable. Then gently breathe out shaping the breath as practised for a count of 3 or 5 whichever you find most comfortable.

When you have finished, take a moment to feel the effects. Do you feel calm and tranquil like the ocean on a sunny summer day?

1. First warm up your shoulders by shrugging them up and down and rotating them backwards and forwards. Gently warm up the wrists by clasping your hands together and gently rotating.

2. Begin by positioning yourself on all fours on the ground, so your body forms a table position. Breathe and imagine being a dolphin in the ocean.

3. Breathing out, lower your elbows to the floor, resting below your shoulder, with your lower arms flat on the ground directly in front of your elbows with your palms faced downwards, fingers slightly splayed like a dolphin's fin

4. Breathing in lift and roll your shoulder blades back, opening your chest. Keep your lower arms flat on the ground. Tuck your toes under, raise your hips skywards by pushing downwards through your arms, upper body, and legs.

Come to a position where your legs are straight, feet flat on the floor. Your back forms a straight line from your hips down towards your head which is flowing down between your forearms. Take a few dolphin breaths here.

If you are struggling to get your legs straight and heels flat on the floor, it is okay to have knees slightly bent and heels off the floor as a beginner.

5. On an out breath gently return your body back to tabletop position. Slowly walk your hands back and bring your body up to a kneeling position, bringing your head up last.

Gently roll out your wrists to release any tension. Breathe and mindfully observe how your body feels.

6. When you are ready you can practice the above again. An alternative lower arm position for no.3 is to clasp the hands together forming a tripod shape with your lower arm.

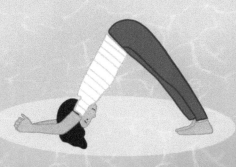

There are many types of meditation, here we explore the meditation of sitting, being present in the moment and allowing our mind to explore being a dolphin.

Start by sitting upright, legs folded in front of you in easy pose. Rest your hands on your lap, palms open upwards or in a mudra.

A mudra is a symbolic gesture, ancient in origin, a positioning of hands or body. Each mudra is said to assist different flows of energy within the body.

A popular mudra used in meditation is the chin mudra. To form the chin mudra, open your palms facing upwards, then fold your index finger and thumb so the tips are touching. This mudra is said to help you connect with your wisdom within.

Begin by breathing gently in and out, allowing your mind and body to settle. When you are ready, close your eyes.

- In your mind's eye imagine you are a beautiful graceful elegant dolphin swimming in the ocean.
- Feel the ocean waves as they glide over your body, cool and invigorating, tingling all your senses with delight.
- Continue to gently breathe in and out. You can breathe in deeply for say a count of 2 or 3 and breathe out slowly for a count of 4 or 5.
- You look around the ocean, everything is calm and tranquil. There is a dazzling array of ocean life flowing in harmony with each other, creating a dancing myriad of rainbow colours.
- You breathe in deeply and out slowly as you flow with the rhythm of the ocean.
- You breathe in the ocean's calm and tranquillity and breathe out any stress.
- Looking up you see rays of golden sunshine shimmering on the ocean surface.
- Everything feels magical, beautiful, and tranquil.
- You stay here for a moment breathing in the beauty and tranquillity of the ocean. You are filled with a feeling of love and bliss.
- When you are ready, slowly open your eyes and return to the present moment sharing a dolphin smile of love with the world.

ACTIVITY
Dancing Star

Dancing Star is a game Crystal and Leo imagined might be played at the underwater party.

Have fun exploring movement and expressions of the underwater world. Dance, move, flow, express yourself in all your magnificence. Then freeze, knowing you are in control of all expressions of the self.

To begin the game, first pick a piece of music you would like to dance to. One person can oversee the music, the DJ.

The rest of the party attendees can have a moment to chat about the party, what it might be like having a party under the sea, what different sea animals might be attending and which sea animal they would like to be etc.

The party begins, the DJ plays the music. Party attendees dance around the room, expressing themselves in freestyle movements.

When the DJ stops the music, dancers freeze in standing Starfish pose.

To get into Starfish pose: -

Dancers stand tall and upright.

They step their feet apart

Their arms stretched up and out - reaching away from the body, with palms open facing frontwards.

Their body grows tall, their head reaching skywards and face forwards with a smile.

When the music starts again, dancers go back into freestyle dance mode, when the music stops, they freeze into Starfish pose, this sequence continues for your chosen time.

(chorus)
Gentle dolphin, gentle dolphin
Swimming the ocean waves
Gently smiling, gently smiling
Sharing your love always

Whatever the weather
Sunshine or rain
Surfing the waves
Is your game.

(chorus)
Gentle dolphin, gentle dolphin
Swimming the ocean waves
Gently smiling, gently smiling
Sharing your love always

Your happy laughter
And happy chatter
Shares ocean music
With all ears.

(chorus)
Gentle dolphin, gentle dolphin
Swimming the ocean waves
Gently smiling, gently smiling
Sharing your love always

Before starting the massage ask your friends permission to massage their back.

1. **Sunrise** – Place fingers on the centre of the back and draw them outwards to the edges of the back in all the different directions, like the rays of the sun.

2. **Shell** – Use tips of fingers to draw shell shapes around the back.

3. **Waves** – Place hands open flat at the base of the spine. Flow hands up the back, with thumbs side by side flowing up the spine. At the top of the spine, hands flow outwards and back down and round to the base of the spine. Repeat this five times.

4. **Splashing** - Place fingers flat on the back and gently tap around the back - like waves splashing.

5. Dolphins – Using finger draw dolphins leaping in and out of the waves.

6. Holding dolphins – place hands over shoulders and give gentle squeezes.

7. Swim to shore – Gently stroke fingers down the back as you swim back to shore.

8. Saying goodbye – Rest hands at the base of the spine as you stand and say goodbye to the dolphins.

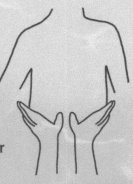

Thank your partner, then repeat above for your partner with their permission.

Corals are living creatures, living in colonies, which build up to form coral reefs. The biggest of which is The Great Barrier Reef located off the coast of Queensland Australia.

The Great Barrier Reef is the world's largest reef system covering 344,400 square kilometres and is the largest living system which can be viewed from space.

Coral reef ecosystems are diverse and complex and home for approximately 10% of the world's fish species.

Reefs play a key role in the health of oceans and subsequently our planet. Oceans cover more than 70% of the earth and provide half the world's oxygen, regulating the global climate system.

Here are some interesting facts on a few of the thousands of species living in the Great Barrier Reef:

- Dolphins are one of the earth's most intelligent creatures. They track using echolocation, inbuilt sonar that bounces sound waves off prey and reveal information like its location, size, and shape.
  They can send and receive sonic frequencies ten times faster than humans, project holographic images and information. A holographic image is like a 3 dimensional photograph.
  Dolphins are semi hemispheric sleepers, which means half of their brain goes to sleep at a time, so that they can keep breathing.
  They have many attributes depicted by humans. Such as their high degree of compassion, often rescuing other animals and humans.
  They are agile, playful and can travel as fast as 35mph.

- Starfish or Sea Star, there are about 2000 different species in all the world's oceans. They are famous for their ability to regenerate limbs, and in some cases, entire bodies.

- Clownfish or Anemonefish, aka Nemo, have around 28 species with a lifespan of 6-10 years. They are hermaphrodites, all born male with the ability to turn themselves female. But once the change is made, they cannot go back to being male. Clownfish are omnivores.

- Sea turtles have roamed the earth's oceans for the last 110 million years, with a lifespan of 50-100 years.

Quiz

1. Which country is the Great Barrier Reef nearest to?
   a) Australia
   b) New Zealand
   c) Tasmania

2. What is the Great Barrier Reef made of?

3. Are Dolphins Fish?

4. What is a mermaid?

5. What is the name of Crystal and Leo's dog?

6. What clever thing can starfish do?

7. Why is it called the Great Barrier Reef?

8. How long have sea turtles been in the earth's oceans?
   a) 50 million years
   b) 110 million years
   c) 750 million years

Answers

1. Australia 2. Living Coral 3. No, they are warm blooded air breathing mammals 4. In folklore stories, mermaid have the upper body of a female human and a tail of a fish. 5. Einstein 6. They can grow back their body parts 7. It covers approx 344,400 square kilometres and is the world's largest reef system. 8. 110 million years.